THIS IS ME! 2022

AMAZING RHYMES

Edited By Andrew Porter

First published in Great Britain in 2022 by:

YoungWriters® Est. 1991

Young Writers
Remus House
Coltsfoot Drive
Peterborough
PE2 9BF
Telephone: 01733 890066
Website: www.youngwriters.co.uk

All Rights Reserved
Book Design by Ashley Janson
© Copyright Contributors 1970
Softback ISBN 978-1-83928-648-3

Printed and bound in the UK by BookPrintingUK
Website: www.bookprintinguk.com
YB0MA0003F

FOREWORD

For Young Writers' latest competition This Is Me, we asked primary school pupils to look inside themselves, to think about what makes them unique, and then write a poem about it! They rose to the challenge magnificently and the result is this fantastic collection of poems in a variety of poetic styles.

Here at Young Writers our aim is to encourage creativity in children and to inspire a love of the written word, so it's great to get such an amazing response, with some absolutely fantastic poems. It's important for children to focus on and celebrate themselves and this competition allowed them to write freely and honestly, celebrating what makes them great, expressing their hopes and fears, or simply writing about their favourite things. This Is Me gave them the power of words. The result is a collection of inspirational and moving poems that also showcase their creativity and writing ability.

I'd like to congratulate all the young poets in this anthology, I hope this inspires them to continue with their creative writing.

CONTENTS

Argyle Primary School, Camden

Maryam Torofdar (9) — 1

Barnes Junior School, Sunderland

Shake Islam (9)	2
Elijah Poulton (8)	3
Lily Mckenzie (10)	4
Oliver Georgou (10)	5
David Minelga (8)	6
Lucas Cole (11)	7

Benhurst Primary School, Elm Park

Danny Vizbaras (11) — 8

Brighton Avenue Primary School, Gateshead

Safa Ali (9)	10
Autumn Tipling (9)	11

Cedars Manor School, Harrow

Husna Sadat (10)	12
Mokhless Khan (9)	13
Yunus Sharifi (9)	14
Abdui Rahman Nabezadeh (10)	15

Christ The Sower Ecumenical Primary School (VA), Milton Keynes

Nafisa Arafat (10)	16
Nafisa Arafat (9)	18

Ariela Ididi	19
Adonaya Armah-Hayford (10)	20
Chrisiah Aasmoah (8)	21
Danita Alill (10)	22

Coddington CE Primary And Nursery School, Coddington

Jessica Shepherd (9)	23
Jessica Dowse (9)	24
Archie Eskriett (9)	26
Florence Bunkle (9)	28
Katie Driver (9)	30

Colneis Junior School, Felixstowe

Mathilda Smith (11)	32
Colby Penston (11)	33
Quinn Smith (11)	34

Eveline Day School, Tooting

Evelyn Ten (9)	35
Eira Whyte (9)	36
Jayden Renner (7)	37

Fairchildes Primary School, New Addington

Dylann Malingo Moffah (10)	38
Denning Moffah (7)	39

Fairview Community Primary School, Wigmore

Sophie Moore (11) — 40

Fulbrook Middle School, Woburn Sands

Molly Fleckney — 41
Hollie Ginger (10) — 42
Ophelia — 43

Gosberton Academy, Gosberton

Austin George Clarke (8) — 44
Jack Lawrence (10) — 45
Roelan Rishan (7) — 46
Macey Watson (7) — 47
Francesca Lawrence (7) — 48

Greenhill Academy, Glodwick

Manahil Ghouse (7) — 49
Muhammad Hussain (7) — 50

Harris Primary Academy Haling Park, Croydon

Tyler Matthews (7) — 51

Hartlebury CE Primary School, Hartlebury

Mitchell Davies (10) — 52
Spencer Brough (9) — 53

Haughton St Giles CE Primary Academy, Haughton

Emelia Allen (9) — 54
Harry Marsh (9) — 55
Charlotte Power (10) — 56

Heathfield School, Rishworth

Roman Wallace (8) — 57
Lucas Giles (8) — 58

Heronsgate School, Walnut Tree

Jamal Khanye (11) — 59
Azaelia Smith (8) — 60
Mattia Ramaj (8) — 62
Sami Ali (9) — 63
Abdulkarim Dandachi (9) — 64

High Greave Junior School, Rotherham

Chelsea Phillips (11) — 65

Hunters Hall Primary School, Dagenham

Yisheng Li (9) — 66
Yaseen Karim (10) — 67
Luca Atonoaei — 68
Sophia Hopkin (8) — 69
Mihadur Rahman (11) — 70
Jenson Sellick (9) — 71
James Baker (9) — 72

Khalsa (VA) Primary School, Southall

Avimannat Kaur (8) — 73

Kirkton Primary School, Carluke

Sophia O'Hare (9) — 74
Gordon Norrie (9) — 75
Molly Elliot (9) — 76

Mereside CE Primary Academy, Shrewsbury

Paige Wilde (7)	77
Raphael Squire (8)	78
Holly Thelwell (8)	79
Ellis Woods (8)	80
Ella Connor (8)	81
Harry Coss (7)	82
Jude White (7)	83
Nathaniel-Graham Richards (9)	84
Ruben Hill Dodd (8)	85

Middleton Parish Church School, Middleton

Oscar Walker (10)	86
James Zakari (10)	87
Harriet Fletcher (10)	88
Leah Cowen (10)	89
Liam Beattie (10)	90
Theo Atkin (10)	91

Oakington Manor Primary School, Wembley

Diyani Vekeria (10)	92

Old Clee Primary Academy, Grimsby

Farrah Robinson (10)	93
Mylie-Rose Robertson (11)	94
Connie-Sue Walker (11)	95
Grace Peart	96
Ashton-Jack Newbegun (10)	97

Our Lady Of Sorrows RC Primary School, Armthorpe

Mollie Russell (8)	98

Sharples Primary School, Bolton

Hashir Mahmood (9)	99
Blake Openshaw (9)	100
Aaminah Adam (9)	101
Dixon Henry (9)	102

St Edmund's RC Primary School, Bungay

Rebecca Plumb (9)	103
Toby Bryant (8)	104

St James' CE Primary School, Oldbury

Khadijah Sambou (10)	106
Bradley Yates (9)	107
Denzel Washington (10)	108
Akaalroop Singh (10)	109
Milo Alvarez (10)	110
Antoni Oslawski (10)	111

St John's Primary School, Liverpool

Ollie Rowtandson (10)	112
Roman Masterson (9)	114
Kristina Pivkova (9)	115
Mandy Hudson (10)	116
Joseph Evans (10)	117
Ruby Cuddy (9)	118
Theodore Ng (10)	119
Maneli Hashemi (9)	120
Aidan Jennings (10)	121
Riley Madden (10)	122
Freya Cashman (11)	123

St Joseph's Catholic Primary School, Haywards Heath

Mia Tongson (8)	124
Anold Johnson (9)	126
Florence Leppard (10)	127
Luis Charlton (8)	128

Jyothika Banesh (11)	129
Alice Hartin (10)	130
Luke Singanallur (10)	131
Sophie Duncan (10)	132
Keeran Espinosa (11)	133
Kevin Mathew Lukose (9)	134

St Joseph's Catholic Primary School, Deptford

Arabella Luyimbazi (9)	135
Summer Pham (9)	136
Izuchukwu Ohanenye (10)	137

St Mark's CE Primary School, Swanage

Tom Suttle (8)	138
Ivy Rose Goode (7)	139
Bradley Wellman (7)	140

St Mary's CE Primary School, Willesden

Ahmad Akbar (10)	141
Riley Ranger (10)	142

St Mary's Primary School, Larkhall

Olivia Michie (9)	143

St Nicholas CE Primary School, Henstridge

Lily Bailey (9)	144
Oliver Traves (9)	145
Zachary Peckover (8)	146
Logan Sunley (8)	147

St Peter's CE Primary School, South Weald

Karl Herber (10)	148
Sienna Neroni (11)	149
Carlotta Strachan (11)	150
Alfie Kinnear (10)	151
Henry Greenwood (9)	152
Sienna Kinnear (9)	153
George Hirst (9)	154
Lola Llewellyn (11)	155
Jenna Shaybany (11)	156
Jaydon Purewal (10)	157
Sonny McCarthy-Whitrod (9)	158

The Bluecoat School, Stamford

Joshua Harrison (10)	159
James Eason (9)	160
Lawrence Buckingham (10)	161
Adi Siwik (10)	162
Audrey Mugonda (10)	163
Tegan Pell (10)	164
Macee Edwards-Jensen (10)	165
Isaac Cowper (11)	166
Kohle De Havilland (10)	167

Thomas Whitehead CE Academy, Houghton Regis

Jayden Barnes (9)	168
Crystal Hall (8)	169
Harry Benson-Coleman (7)	170

Trinity Academy, Richmond

Rhys Bennett (8)	171

Valley Invicta Primary School At East Borough, Maidstone

Abdullah Qumi (8)	172

Wilberlee Junior & Infant School, Wilberlee

Oliver Zahoor (10) 173
Isaac Bennett (11) 174

Wymondham College, Morley

Doyinsola Abdul-Obitayo (12) 175

THE POEMS

Turn That Frown Upside Down

When I'm down
I just want to wait, for a second of reflection
I think I did my best, so let's keep that in our hearts
But even if you're not shining, like the evening star
You've always got something in your heart
And I'll tell you what that is
Your unique self
So, one, two, three, go
Be you
Never give up
Try your best to get up to the top.

Maryam Torofdar (9)
Argyle Primary School, Camden

Happy Is Fun

Happy is fun
It's all fun and games
We have fun when you're happy
You play all day
Fun is good
When playing with someone it is fun
It makes you happy
It's fun when you play at school
You talk to your friends
At home you spend time with your family
It's all fun and games
When you're happy you play a lot
We have fun
We have fun.

Shake Islam (9)
Barnes Junior School, Sunderland

This Is Me

E nergetic
L oving
I ntelligent
J oyful
A nxious
H elpful

H elpful
Y ummy
R espectful
U seful
I maginative

P atient
O ptimistic
U nderstanding
L ikeable
T enacious
O bedient
N urturing.

Elijah Poulton (8)
Barnes Junior School, Sunderland

Snazzy

Sporty
Swifty, energetic
Challenging, daring, exciting
Always ready to do something
Challenging

Arty
Creative, hard-working
Creating, crafting, painting
Always drawing planets
Artist

Funny
Energetic, humorous
Amusing, entertaining, diverting
Always making people laugh
Hilarious.

Lily Mckenzie (10)
Barnes Junior School, Sunderland

It's Just Me

Energetic
Funny, pleasant
Interesting, running, jumping
Always ready for a challenge
Lively

Inspiring
Clever, intelligent
Teaching, learning, thinking
Always ready to learn new things
Motivating.

Oliver Georgou (10)
Barnes Junior School, Sunderland

Fortnite Kings

Fortnite is...
A game
Makes me happy
Burns time
Gives me a laugh
You can make friends
A fun game
I love it
I enjoy it.

David Minelga (8)
Barnes Junior School, Sunderland

Me!

Me!
Artistic, lazy!
Sleeping, running, amazing!
A masterpiece by God!
Kind!

Lucas Cole (11)
Barnes Junior School, Sunderland

I Am Me

I am me,
I like animals
I like food,
And so on,

I am me,
I like dogs,
I like frogs,
And so on,

I am me,
I like potatoes,
I like tomatoes,
And so on,

I am me,
I like family,
I like sports,
And so on,

I am me,
I love my dad,

I love my mum,
And so on,

I am me,
I like skiing,
I like basketball,
And so on,

I am me,
I like skiing,
I like basketball
And so on,

I am me,
You are you,
We are friends,
Forever.

Danny Vizbaras (11)
Benhurst Primary School, Elm Park

My Emotions In One

My sadness is as blue as a sea on a stormy night,
My loneliness is as white as snow,
My anger is as red as a huge fire,
My darkness is a pit of pitch black in a hole,
My powerful life is as green as acid,
My love is as yellow as a daffodil,
My happiness is as gold as the sun,
My heart is as bright as the sun,
My caring is as colourful as a rainbow.

Safa Ali (9)
Brighton Avenue Primary School, Gateshead

My Colours Are Motion!

My silliness is green as grass.
My happiness is as yellow as sunshine.
My sadness is like a red rose.
My love is pink as a cloud in the sky.
My gloominess is black as a cloud.
My colours are the rainbow in the sky.

Autumn Tipling (9)
Brighton Avenue Primary School, Gateshead

This Is Me

T his is me, built fine the way I am.
H usna is my name, and I love jam.
I 'm mostly a comedian, definitely independent.
S uper fun to hang around with, and I'm awesome!

I am patient, sometimes smart,
S ince I'm intelligent, I'd like to become a teacher.

M aybe I'm rude, but I'm known to be friendly,
E ven though I'm organised, I'm still mostly messy!

Husna Sadat (10)
Cedars Manor School, Harrow

This Is Me

I'm sporty and a little naughty
I really love cats and I always use taps
I love to draw and have fun
I like to play and I like to run
My favourite lesson is PE
Maths and ICT
I'm a really good striker
And I love to score
The football field is as green as an emerald
When I lay I feel like a general
I'm a great friend and son
And I really like to have fun!

Mokhless Khan (9)
Cedars Manor School, Harrow

Me

In my room,
I like to draw,
I like to play,
As it makes my day,
When I see a ball,
I kick it to the wall.

My room's messy,
Because I'm lazy,
I'm focused on entertainment,
To make sure I'm not bored.

I like maths,
But usually,
I'm stuck to my device.

Yunus Sharifi (9)
Cedars Manor School, Harrow

This Is Me!

My favourite animal,
Can you guess what it is?
Its claws are like kitchen knives,
Don't go near this creature,
As its claws are its best feature!
It has teeth like razor blades,
And doesn't like lying in shade,
One last clue,
It has brown fur.
What is it?

Abdui Rahman Nabezadeh (10)
Cedars Manor School, Harrow

The Earth Is Dying...

I'm funny,
I'm silly,
I'm amazing and amusing,
But mostly me,
I'm weird and jolly,
I'm crazy,
I'm lazy,
But there's one thing I'm the most,
I care for a frightful environment,
Which hasn't been,
Well cared for,
We're littering,
We're smoking,
We're vaping,
We're polluting,
Our Earth is dying,
And no one is helping,
A few volunteers,
Is all we need,
Just stand and,
Give me a chance,

The koalas are dying,
The trees are dying,
The animals are dying,
The Earth is dying...

Nafisa Arafat (10)
Christ The Sower Ecumenical Primary School (VA), Milton Keynes

This Is Me!

I'm caring,
I'm kind,
And I love animals,
(Especially rabbits and reptiles,)
Netball is my passion,
It's a game I like to play,
People say I'm good that's what they say,
When I shoot the ball,
My legs thump as I jump
When I'm doing art
I always eat a tart
I'm part of The Cray Team
Which are my best friends
I'm grateful to have them that's what I say say.

Nafisa Arafat (9)
Christ The Sower Ecumenical Primary School (VA), Milton Keynes

All About Me

A lways playing Roblox twenty-four-seven
R eally looking forward to get high grades
I am a kind, caring friend looking out for people.
E lsa and Anna were my favourites when I was little.
L ife is sometimes when you add a lot of pressure.
A lways showing school values: compassion, respect, friendship.

Ariela Ididi
Christ The Sower Ecumenical Primary School (VA), Milton Keynes

All About Me

Adonaya is my name
I love snow and art
I'm pretty smart
I love red velvet cake
And I love to bake
I'm cool
I'm fun
I get along with everyone
I have two sisters who are annoying
And lame
I have good friends
I have a good brain
I like playing games
This is me.

Adonaya Armah-Hayford (10)
Christ The Sower Ecumenical Primary School (VA), Milton Keynes

This Is Me

T iny as my size
H aving my family on my back
I love me and my family
S hine bright like a beautiful star.

I am lovely and my family,
S tar like shine night.

M eant to be cheerful
E njoy and cheerful and happy.

Chrisiah Aasmoah (8)
Christ The Sower Ecumenical Primary School (VA), Milton Keynes

Danita
A kennings poem

I am a...

Book reader
Badminton player
Maths solver
Family lover
K-Pop listener
Animal hugger
And forever
A kind helper.

Danita Alill (10)
Christ The Sower Ecumenical Primary School (VA), Milton Keynes

My Magic Box
(Based on 'Magic Box' by Kit Wright)

I will put in my box,
Loud neighing horses in posh stables and beautiful greys
Snoozing on the soft, flat straw.

I will put in my box,
Delicious scrumptious hay in the brightest hay nets you could imagine
And drizzling water in bright purple buckets.

I will put in my box
You and your horse in the freezing shivering cold air
In the winter without coats.

I will put in my box
Children riding the best-trained horses
And taking care of the five-star light chestnut horses.

My box is transformed,
From a boring wooden box to a multicoloured box
With magical secrets in every corner.

Jessica Shepherd (9)
Coddington CE Primary And Nursery School, Coddington

My Magic Box
(Based on 'Magic Box' by Kit Wright)

I will put in my box,
Sun shining in the sky and clouds looming,
Flowers blooming,
Hear the birds chirping and singing,
Feel the breeze of the summer wind reflecting on your face.

I will put in my box,
Rainy, cold Easter days,
Chicks blossoming, lambs feeding,
Hunt for eggs,
See the opposite of sad on even your cat.

I will put in my box,
The sweet sound of leaves crunching,
Trick or treat,
Soon it will be Halloween night!
Pumpkins getting carved because it's autumn, yeah, right.

I will put in my box,
Christmas pudding scent filling the room,

Fireworks flying and soaring up in the sky,
Snow falling,
Getting smudged up while you're cuddling up.

My box has leaves fluttering,
Flowers springing on top of my box,
Made from white stuff like snow,
But lastly, a golden butterfly surrounded by flowers.

I shall watch,
The colours of autumn in the sky,
April drops floating and dripping all over the place,
Summer's sun shining in my eye,
Winter's vibe of cold breath, ice,
I will have all the seasons in my box.

Jessica Dowse (9)
Coddington CE Primary And Nursery School, Coddington

My Magic Box

(Based on 'Magic Box' by Kit Wright)

I will put in my box,
A unicorn from the lost world,
The juice from an apple tree,
And the lovely taste of chips.

I will put in my box
Some sweet treats,
A teddy bear,
And the swag of a dog's tail.

I will put in my box,
Some clothes of the latest fashion,
A box of puppies
And some snow falling from the sky.

I will put in my box,
A big T-rex,
Some cupcakes,
And a water tank.

I will put in my box,
A PS5,

The wildest sloth,
And a book.

I will put in my box,
A nice bear,
The honey bees,
And a book.

I will put in my box,
A tiger,
A three-leaf clove,
And £1,000,000,000 in cash.

I will put in my box,
A wolf,
A sloth,
And the Eiffel Tower.

I will put in my box,
Seven tins of Match Attax
An iPhone,
And a diamond.

Archie Eskriett (9)
Coddington CE Primary And Nursery School, Coddington

My Magic Box
(Based on 'Magic Box' by Kit Wright)

In my magic box,
I will put Pandora's cry as she opens the chest,
All the evil in the world,
And a tiny speck of hope.

In my magic box,
I will put all illness back where it belongs,
The cackle of the creator,
And the villainous varieties of criminals.

In my magic box,
I will put the never-ending wars of the world,
All death, destruction and damage,
And the cries of distress like shrieking mice.

My magic box was created by mythology
Its frame is made from flimsy wood
The hinges are made out of pure darkness and gloom
Its lid shines with stars as the sun comes over the horizon.

I shall spread the hope in my box and bring the horrors joy,
Lightness grows as I pass through and Pandora's cry will fade.

Florence Bunkle (9)
Coddington CE Primary And Nursery School, Coddington

My Magic Box

(Based on 'Magic Box' by Kit Wright)

I will put in my box,
The swish of the dark blue sea waves,
The swish of a silk sari on a summer night,
The swish of the ghost in the night.

I will put in my box,
The special day when I first held my brother, George,
The special day when my mum and dad held me for the first time,
The amazing time when I first looked in a loud wolf's dark eyes, which glittered in the glamorous night.

I will put in my box,
Three magic wishes from the mysterious fire dragon in New York City,
An elk doing a murmer,
When I'm in my box, I will do a backflip off a beam.

My box is fashioned with sparkly sparkles,
It's purple with pink in the corners,
And it's got snowflakes on the lid.

Katie Driver (9)
Coddington CE Primary And Nursery School, Coddington

This Is Me

I am an
Art lover
I get A+ on all my answers
Wait... this isn't me
This is who I want to be
This is me...
A pet lover
A blue-eyed character
A tennis player
A pasta lover
Hot countries are my place to be
I will always be there for my friends
Even if the friendship ends
Now this is me.

Mathilda Smith (11)
Colneis Junior School, Felixstowe

Fruit Bowl

I'm an orange -
A smooth, juicy orange,
I was in an orchard,
Hanging from its branches,
Living above the peaches,
My life was an adventure,
Through joy and happiness,
But now I'm in a fruit bowl,
I feel like my body's leaving my soul,
Sometimes I'm distracted,
My life, I feel like I act it.

Colby Penston (11)
Colneis Junior School, Felixstowe

I Am A

I am a...
Kind, happy, joyful,
Full of energy,
Book reading, caring,
Funny, smart, forgiving,
Fun, quiet, good friend,
Cheerful, light-hearted,
Crazy, silly, gleeful,
Joyous, sweet, understanding,
Unselfish, sympathetic,
Foolish, wild, sunny,
Person.

Quinn Smith (11)
Colneis Junior School, Felixstowe

This Is Who I Am

I am sometimes shy
And I might come by to say hi
I can come in grey, black or ginger
I don't like being poked by a finger
I can sometimes scratch if you're not my match
I like to play with bouncy balls
And I listen to my owner's calls
I am mostly lazy and sometimes crazy
And if you don't give me food I become a little rude
And I can change my mood
If you stroke my fur
You'll definitely be able to hear me purr...

This is me.

Evelyn Ten (9)
Eveline Day School, Tooting

What Is It?

An animal of land, sea and the sky,
Has wings and can fly,
They like weeds and bread,
They like it when they're fed,
They're green, brown and a hint of yellow,
They are usually a nice fellow,
When they're in water it's a pond,
I'm sure they like to bond,
On land they waddle,
But in water they're like a model.
What is it?

Answer: A duck.

Eira Whyte (9)
Eveline Day School, Tooting

What Am I?

I have pincers and I am poisonous.
I live in deserts.
I eat small, green insects.
I am a predator.
I have battles with other bugs.
I have a tail.
I have big pincers.
I have claws on my mouth.
What am I?

Answer: I am a scorpion.

Jayden Renner (7)
Eveline Day School, Tooting

I, Me And Myself

I'm good at maths and literacy,
Also, science and history,
An arty boy with creativity,
That boy, you might have guessed, is me,
I like to draw and doodle all the time,
I also know how to make poems rhyme,
Do you know many facts about space?
I know things all over the place!
That is it, can't you see?
I'd like to end this poem with,
This is me.

Dylann Malingo Moffah (10)
Fairchildes Primary School, New Addington

Myself

I always act like a teacher
Because I am clever
I like computing and TV
As it builds my curiosity
I hate getting told off
Or else it will be fixed with hugs and sweet stuff
Even though I am the shy type
I am as happy as a child
I like alphabets
With new sets.

Denning Moffah (7)
Fairchildes Primary School, New Addington

I Am Who I Am

I might not be the most beautiful
I might not be your first choice
But that's cool, because I am who I am
I will use my own voice

Through the tough and the easy
Eventually, I will rejoice
About who I am and what I enjoy
I am who I am, with no regrets
This is my choice!

Sophie Moore (11)
Fairview Community Primary School, Wigmore

Squishy

I like to squish my squishies in the morning.
I like to squish my squishies at lunch.
But I love to squish my squishies at night,
When I am tucked up in bed all tight.
My squishies are very naughty,
They jump up on the sofa,
And the sofa and throw the pillows off.
They like to make a lot of noise,
Until they get told to stop.
My cat gets really angry,
And sways them in the face,
My dog gets really scared,
And runs away like he's in a race.

Molly Fleckney
Fulbrook Middle School, Woburn Sands

A Recipe For Hollie

If I were a recipe,
This is what I'd be,
Split into two cups,
One for you and the other for me.
A little bit of flour,
A sprinkle of salt,
Two little eggs,
And some chocolate to melt.
Put them all together,
1, 2, 3... add a little happiness,
And you have me.

Hollie Ginger (10)
Fulbrook Middle School, Woburn Sands

This Is Me

This is me.
I love skiing,
Fresh, fast, free.

I love kickboxing and climbing,
The rush of climbing up the steady walls,
And the strength of punching the bags.

I am always happy,
Inside and out,
I am always going to be me.

Ophelia
Fulbrook Middle School, Woburn Sands

All About Me And Your Sister

We are all special
We are all different it's true
But what is the difference between me and you?

You can do gymnastics
While I can play football
And when the day is done we both like to cuddle

You like raspberries, while I like apples
But both of us love to eat juicy strawberries

My har is brown and your hair is blonde
I get up quite early while you stay in bed

We'll be siblings forever, no day will it end
We may be different but you are my best friend.

Austin George Clarke (8)
Gosberton Academy, Gosberton

My Dog

Underneath my outside face
There's a face that none can see,
A little less smiley
A little less sure,
But a whole lot more like me.

I eat my peas with honey.
I've done it all my life.
It makes the peas taste funny
But it keeps them on the knife!

I am a dog.
You are a flower.
I lift my leg up
And give you a shower!

Jack Lawrence (10)
Gosberton Academy, Gosberton

Roelan

R unning too fast? Sorry, it's what I do
O f course I am the best gamer
E nergy fills me like food
L earning, playing and football are my favourites
A nimation videos like cartoon beatbox battles are my favourite
N o one is faster than me.

Roelan Rishan (7)
Gosberton Academy, Gosberton

Mad About Minecraft

My name is Macey
I like to play Minecraft
Creepers like to face me
They make me laugh
I love a cup of tea
When breaking wood in half
Minecraft is the best you see
I wish they had a giraffe
I play it on my Switch
In Minecraft, I'm super rich!

Macey Watson (7)
Gosberton Academy, Gosberton

Francesca Likes...

I like to cheer and dance
I like to prance and prance
I like to drink a cup of tea
I like to stroke my doggy
I like to run around
I like to jump like a froggy
These are some of my likes in life
To be happy, smile and do things right.

Francesca Lawrence (7)
Gosberton Academy, Gosberton

A Kennings Poem About Me
A kennings poem

Bad drawer
Family lover
Sleeping lover
Amazing singer.

Fidget player
Man Utd supporter
Rubbish thrower
Slow runner.

Slime lover
Ride hater
Shopping lover
Trip taker.

Manahil Ghouse (7)
Greenhill Academy, Glodwick

Acrostic Poem

M athematician
U nderestimated
H eroic
A spiring
M arvellous
M ajestic
A ccomplished
D aring.

Muhammad Hussain (7)
Greenhill Academy, Glodwick

Poem About Me

T rees are nice because they give us air.
Y ellow makes me feel happy.
L ight makes everything shine.
E llie makes me feel happy because she is nice.
R eindeer make people happy.

Tyler Matthews (7)
Harris Primary Academy Haling Park, Croydon

The Great Me

I'm a boxer.
The heavy breathing when the bags roar,
Pushing myself to my limits,
When my coach says twenty-second blast go,
Never giving up. Never stop trying. Never say no.

I am a gamer.
Concentrating on the screen, never even blinking,
Straight face of determination always trying to win,
My fingers move faster than the speed of light trying to hide from other players,
Face of no defeat always as a team.

I am my family.
Always there when I'm stuck,
We always work together, never alone,
We work better as a team,
We concentrate on our target until we complete it.

Mitchell Davies (10)
Hartlebury CE Primary School, Hartlebury

Super Spencer

S pectacular at sports
U nbelievable playing football
P leasant and charming
E normous kindness in my veins
R eluctant at unacceptable, hesitant at evil.

S wift at school
P eaceful and soft
E ye-catching and independent
N oble and obedient
C heerful and pleasing
E nthusiastic and excelling
R espectable and astonishing.

Spencer Brough (9)
Hartlebury CE Primary School, Hartlebury

Busy Bee

This is me,
I'm a nine-year-old busy bee,
I love to learn,
I've got energy to burn,
My eyes are green, my hair is blonde,
I tidy my room with a magic wand,
My pony is called Barry and I'm a horsey girl,
If we see a big jump, we'll give it a whirl,
I can't sit still, I've got ants in my pants,
I run and jump and sing and dance,
You might say I'm quite sporty,
I've lost count but I play about forty,
Tennis and cricket when the sun is out,
Football and swimming when there's snow about,
When the snow is too deep, I read Harry Potter,
I play in the paddling pool when the weather's hotter,
So this is me, as smiley as can be,
I've got to go, Mum's shouting me for tea.

Emelia Allen (9)
Haughton St Giles CE Primary Academy, Haughton

Last-Minute Winner

Every day I see draws and losses,
Now I wonder, will Liverpool win?
The atmosphere at Anfield always is great,
Even waiting for a Klopp-dog,
They smell like the greatest thing ever,
But never will anyone agree,
Except me,
Klopp-dogs taste like victory,
I can almost touch the Premier League trophy,
We've won 4-3 with a last-minute goal from Origi,
So the three points are ours,
And we all shout, "You'll never walk alone!"
It's about the be lifted,
And the League is ours.

Harry Marsh (9)
Haughton St Giles CE Primary Academy, Haughton

Charlotte

Charlotte is my name,
To be a horse rider is my aim,
I bend just like elastic,
I also love gymnastics,
My pony is called Foxy,
But I've never lived in Doxey,
I also have a dog,
Though I'd like a hedgehog,
I have three cats,
But I don't have any bats,
I have seven hens,
And I keep them away from the fox's dens,
I have blonde hair and blue eyes,
But that doesn't make me unwise,
I go to a great school,
Although, sadly, it doesn't have a swimming pool.

Charlotte Power (10)
Haughton St Giles CE Primary Academy, Haughton

Rugby League

R aging game
U p the ball goes
G ood game
B y the way, it's my favourite part
Y es! We won!

L asering kick
E xceptional players
A nd my dad and uncle play it
G ood sportsmanship
U nlikely to get injured
E xceptionally strong.

Roman Wallace (8)
Heathfield School, Rishworth

Lucas

L unatic Lucas
U K is where I live
C alm and courageous
A ctive and a team player
S uper smart.

Lucas Giles (8)
Heathfield School, Rishworth

I Am Jamal Khanye

I am my mum Einath, caring and kind.
I am my dad Bezel, determined to play football.
I am my football coach Sean, who wanted me to do better.
I am my uncle, the mathematician.
I am my aunties, who taught me how to have fun.
I am my friends, who believed in me.
I am my brothers, Xavier and Aiden.
I am my teacher, who says I will succeed.
I am Jamal Khanye, who helped my team in the rocket volley final.
I am who I am because of everyone.

Jamal Khanye (11)
Heronsgate School, Walnut Tree

The Poem

A kind-hearted person, that's me,
Z ay is my nickname, that's me,
A thletic like I'm flexible, that's me,
E ating chocolate is my favourite like I'm dreaming, that's me,
L illy is my best friend, I could never do something without her, that's me,
I dress like a model like I'm famous, that's me,
A person who wants to be a CEO when I'm older, that's me.

"R egister!" I shout when they call my name, that's me,
A fashion designer when I'm older, that's me,
I 'm fashionable with clothes that are black and white, with an adorable smile

S mith is my last name same as my dad that's me
M y family's happy with me but I'm okay with it, that's me,
I 'm a middle child but I don't get much attention as a middle child, that's me,
T ailai just look like my sister, just a friend, we say, "Nice to meet you," that's me,
"H i," I say when someone new, but I don't know you, got in trouble before because I just met you, that's me.

Azaelia Smith (8)
Heronsgate School, Walnut Tree

All About Me

T aller than a small car.
H ave one brother and sister.
I like gaming and watching TV.
S ometimes silly.

I 'm dirty, sometimes I fall in puddles and get dirty.
S illy as a sausage.

M y handwriting is messy.
E nd the school!

Mattia Ramaj (8)
Heronsgate School, Walnut Tree

Angry Me

When I'm angry sometimes
I could kick stuff
And sometimes when I'm not angry
I'll be happy.

Sami Ali (9)
Heronsgate School, Walnut Tree

Ecstatic

To create me you will need
A spoonful of laughter
A gallon of fun
A thousand litres of joy.

Abdulkarim Dandachi (9)
Heronsgate School, Walnut Tree

The Unicorn Poem

A unicorn loves to dance
A donkey likes to prance
The unicorn and donkey met at a park
They became best friends
Until the day came to an end
The next day the donkey and unicorn met again
This time they saw humans
They hid as fast as they could
The children found them
They all became friends.

Chelsea Phillips (11)
High Greave Junior School, Rotherham

If The World Was Water

If the world was water,
I would flush away arguments and moisturise the Earth.
If the world was water,
I would drink happiness giving smiles on sad faces.
Flush every fear, pour every tear, splash every scream.

If the world was water,
I would wash us all to school.
If the world was water,
I could chill every burning flame of raging people.
If the world was water,
I would moisturise the Earth.

All the world is not water,
But I still imagine how lovely it would be.

Yisheng Li (9)
Hunters Hall Primary School, Dagenham

About Me

I don't like maths, I like literacy, I like games on my iPads.
I like this girl not in my class, her name begins with G,
She is flexible, she is sweet, cute, she stole my heart.
Every time she smiles at me I blush.
I wish school was shorter, like three hours, max.
My favourite movies are Tangled and Moana
I love those movies
But my life is boring,
I like the game Minecraft, but I do no not like my life
Because I am not good at anything.

Yaseen Karim (10)
Hunters Hall Primary School, Dagenham

The Day That Happiness Came To Visit

One sunny day I heard a gently knocking door,
Blue eyes, orange clothes, and a vast smile.
When I saw her I felt an enormous happiness.
We discussed and laughed like old friends.
I asked her what to eat and drink.
I gave her an orange and a white wine.
She said to me, "Goodbye," and left me with a smile.
I will wait for happiness to come again.

Luca Atonoaei
Hunters Hall Primary School, Dagenham

Joy

J ust be joyful, jolly and joyful,
O nly think happy thoughts when you're jolly and joyful.
Y elling won't help you if you want to be jolly and joyful.

Sophia Hopkin (8)
Hunters Hall Primary School, Dagenham

I'm The Best

I like to eat pizza!
I like to play football.
My favourite game is Minecraft.
I like PSH.
I like Nike shoes.
My favourite football team is Liverpool.

Mihadur Rahman (11)
Hunters Hall Primary School, Dagenham

Recipe Of Me!

A drizzle of smiles
A sprinkle of funniness
A spoonful of creative
A spot of cheekiness
A cup of joyfulness
This is me!

Jenson Sellick (9)
Hunters Hall Primary School, Dagenham

James

J ust nine years old
A lways writing
M akes others laugh
E xtra hilarious
S uper handsome.

James Baker (9)
Hunters Hall Primary School, Dagenham

All About Your Best

If you always try your best
Then you'll never have to wonder
About what you could have done.
If you summoned all your thunder
And if your best was not as good
As you hoped it would be
You still could say, "I gave today all that I had in me."
People also call me mindful and polite.

Avimannat Kaur (8)
Khalsa (VA) Primary School, Southall

This My Dog!

L una is my lovely dog out of all dogs but she is a type of dangerous dog.
U sually she's a bit cranky but she's nice to my dad more, that's not fair.
N ow she might have puppies we're not sure but we are excited but she now protects herself.
A t last she's adorable as well she loves tomatoes more than anything, woof woof this is Luna!

Sophia O'Hare (9)
Kirkton Primary School, Carluke

This Is Me

I am the creative god
Look at me with the fishing rod
Yeah I am as cunning as a ninja
Look at this person that's gonna pinch ya
I'm as sensitive as a pig gonna catch ya
I'm as smart as Einstein
Not as dumb as a porcupine
I'm as speedy like a cheetah
I can drink a full litre.

Gordon Norrie (9)
Kirkton Primary School, Carluke

This Is Buddy

   B oy
o **U** tstanding
   D efinitely good
   D elightful
   Y ou are the funniest, cutset cat of all!

I love you so much!

Molly Elliot (9)
Kirkton Primary School, Carluke

How To Make Me

Ingredients you will need

A sparkle of prettiness
A handful of stories
A slab of delicious chocolate cake
3kg of fun, love and funniness
A dash of friendship
A dash of love for my brother
A dash of Disney movies
A teaspoon of sweetness

Now you will need to

First add a sparkle of prettiness.
Secondly, add a handful of stories.
Next, add a slab of delicious chocolate cake.
Fourth, 3kg of fun, love and funniness.
Fifth, add a dash of friendship.
Sixth, add a dash of love for my brother.
Seventh, add a dash of Disney movies.
Lastly, add a teaspoon of sweetness and mix it together
And put me in the oven for 1 hour.

Paige Wilde (7)
Mereside CE Primary Academy, Shrewsbury

How To Make Raphael

Ingredients
A sprinkle of Fortnite
A spoonful of silliness
A pinch of sadness
A slab of pepperoni pizza
A dash of sunlight and
A gaming bedroom

You will need to...!
Add a spoonful of silliness
Mix in a gaming room
Stir roughly while adding a slab of pepperoni pizza
Next, add a pinch of sadness and
A dash of sunlight.
Spread the mix neatly over the tray with baking paper.
Cook until glazed and fun-filled bubbles can be seen.
Add a sprinkle of Fortnite
Now wait to cool down.

This is me!

Raphael Squire (8)
Mereside CE Primary Academy, Shrewsbury

How To Make Me

Ingredients:
An overload of Roblox
A pinch of Minecraft
A slab of internet
A sprinkle of teddy bears
A spoonful of blonde happiness
A spoonful of ice cubes
A dash of Disneyland
A slab of glitter

Method:
Mix Roblox crazy while adding Minecraft
Crush the teddy bears and
Add the Internet
Carefully add 1 blonde happiness strand
Add all of your ice cubs
Put in Disneyland and
Stop mixing and add the glitter.

Holly Thelwell (8)
Mereside CE Primary Academy, Shrewsbury

A Recipe For Me

Ingredients
A dash of KFC
A spoonful of Fortnite
A slab of pizza
30g of football
A pinch of ice cream
A cup of steaming hot chocolate

Method
First, take a dash of KFC
After that, add 30g of football
Next, mix in a spoonful of Fortnite
Then stir in a slab of pizza and a pinch of ice cream
Put it into a tray and pour over a cup of hot chocolate
Pour it into the oven and bake.

Ellis Woods (8)
Mereside CE Primary Academy, Shrewsbury

All About Me

E ight is my age.
L ouise is my middle name.
L ike food so much.
A xolotls are my third favourite animal.

C onnor is my last name.
O reos are my favourite biscuit.
N ever call me Ellie.
N ovember 6th is my birthday.
O livia is my friend.
R eally love surface pressure.

Ella Connor (8)
Mereside CE Primary Academy, Shrewsbury

How To Make Me

3 hours of Fortnite
3 litres of gaming
A friend called Alfie
A friend called Jack
A bit of cheekiness

First, you add together 3 litres of gaming and a friend called Jack.
Then add a slab of cheese.
Now add a friend called Alfie.
Then add 3 hours of Fortnite.
Finally, add a bit of cheekiness.

Harry Coss (7)
Mereside CE Primary Academy, Shrewsbury

All About Me

J oel is my best friend
U mbrellas keep me dry
D og is my favourite pet
E very Friday I play football

W illiam is my best friend
H arry is my best friend
I love football
T ate is my best friend
E very Saturday I watch my sister play football.

Jude White (7)
Mereside CE Primary Academy, Shrewsbury

Nathaniel

N oodles are my favourite food
A be is my best friend
T rains are my favourite transport
H arry is my best friend
A can of Coca-Cola
N ine is how old I am
I love my Jurassic World game
E llis is my best friend
L ions are my favourite animals.

Nathaniel-Graham Richards (9)
Mereside CE Primary Academy, Shrewsbury

This Is Me

My name is Ruben and I like rugby,
I like going to rugby with my dad,
Rugby is a sport that I like,
I love it so much,
I want to play rugby when I'm older.

Ruben Hill Dodd (8)
Mereside CE Primary Academy, Shrewsbury

How I Am Unique

Once upon a time
I wrote a great rhyme
Which was all about me
And how I am unique

I love to be lazy
But I am also very crazy
I am a football lover
And I have dogs too
And if I think hard enough
I love the cows that go moo

I shine like a rainbow
Like an angel with a halo
I have bright blue eyes
And a smile that shines

I wish to be an author
Maybe even a footballer
I dream to have two dogs
As I sleep like a log.

Oscar Walker (10)
Middleton Parish Church School, Middleton

Another Day's Life

F antastic football is fantastic as it teaches, you about the qualities in life
O bedience, football teaches you to listen to your coach
O ffence in football, I play the offence position
T -shirt, I normally wear a Man United T-shirt
B oost, I wear football boots to hit the ball hard and score
A chievements, I have achieved and won trophies and medals
L ionel Messi is my icon and hero
L ucky Lingard saved United against West Ham.

James Zakari (10)
Middleton Parish Church School, Middleton

Happy Harriet

Harriet is my name
And a chef is my aim
I have a big brother
A mum and a dad
My behaviour is never bad
Sade, the brilliant, is my best friend
I know our friendship will never end

I'm pretty smart
And I love art
I'm kinda crazy
And really lazy

My skin is soft and white
And my hair is brown and light
I have really light freckles
People say that they make me special

So that is me
I hope you're happy.

Harriet Fletcher (10)
Middleton Parish Church School, Middleton

All About Me!

I'm kind and true
Just like you
I'm loving and bright
All things nice
I love dogs and cats
And that's one of my facts

My friends are kind
But sometimes are hard to find
I love spicy curry
But sometimes my parents are in a hurry

This is me!

Leah Cowen (10)
Middleton Parish Church School, Middleton

My Dream

I plan to be a doctor
Maybe a surgeon
I know it would be hard
But this is my dream
So I would take the job
I like to be helpful
So this is the job for me
This is my dream
So I hope I get it
Because it will make me happy.

Liam Beattie (10)
Middleton Parish Church School, Middleton

This Is Me!

T iny as an ant
H elpful as a clock
E xcellent Theo is an intelligent elephant
O bsessed with football ad video games - this is me.

Theo Atkin (10)
Middleton Parish Church School, Middleton

Me And I

Diyani is my name,
I am as stunning as a star,
My aim is to be wiser,
My favourite thing to do is to do more homework,
I am like a moon shining across the sky,
My mum and dad make me feel better when I'm down,
I love them so much,
And they love me back.

    D elightful at school and at home!
    I nspired to be anything I want to be
    Y ou learn when you are at school
    A dorable
    N ature lover
    I ndependent.

Diyani Vekeria (10)
Oakington Manor Primary School, Wembley

The Book That Makes Me Happy

H ermione is the smartest of the trio.
A nyone can go to Hogwarts.
R on is the funny member of the trio.
R eading is Hermione's favourite thing to do.
Y axley was a Death Eater.

P otter is Draco's enemy.
O nly Harry took time to set Dobby free.
T ogether the trio defeated Voldemort.
T onight we celebrate their victory.
E very day Harry was the bravest.
R ight away Hagrid helped Harry.

Farrah Robinson (10)
Old Clee Primary Academy, Grimsby

Features

My features
My features are as unique as
Every individual shell that gets washed
Up on shore.

Freckles that bloom in the summer sun
Like fresh daisies, each one as distinct as each other.

Eyes as blue as the bright ocean waves
Glassy like windows, you can see straight through
Them.

Features
Not everyone's is the same...

Mylie-Rose Robertson (11)
Old Clee Primary Academy, Grimsby

What's Inside Of Us?

Trees are natural,
Cars are man-made,
The hearts inside us should last a decade,
Our organs wriggle and jiggle,
Whereas a kid's drawing is just a scribble,
Our bones are solid,
While some toddlers are stolid,
That's what's inside our body,
Including when we go potty.

Connie-Sue Walker (11)
Old Clee Primary Academy, Grimsby

Just Me

I look in the mirror,
And what do I see,
I see the me,
That no one else can be.

I'm precious,
I'm glad to be me,
My hair, my face,
My personality.

My size, my shape,
The colour of my skin,
All that makes me up,
My outsides and in.

Grace Peart
Old Clee Primary Academy, Grimsby

Be Happy

I give people a spring in their step,
I really don't like to see people upset,
When everyone is happy the world is a better place,
Looking around, seeing everyone with a smile on their face,
Never be rusty, always be nice,
Everybody wants to live a happy life.

Ashton-Jack Newbegun (10)
Old Clee Primary Academy, Grimsby

This Is Me

I am a cat, playful and brave,
I am a lover of singing inside, not outside,
I am a horse, fast and graceful in a garden,
My eyes are as shiny as a star in the sky,
My hair is as black as a dark night,
This is me.

Mollie Russell (8)
Our Lady Of Sorrows RC Primary School, Armthorpe

This Is Me

I am as silly as a penguin,
I am a child who is fast as a panther,
At night, my anger is fiery orange.
In the morning, my heart is as yellow as a sunflower.
I am as valiant as a tiger being a sidekick,
I am as radiant as a snake,
I am as radioactive as Spider-Man.
This is me!

Hashir Mahmood (9)
Sharples Primary School, Bolton

This Is Blake

Blake is the best at PVZ
I have practised all day long
But I can't get my eyes off it
A little minute on it
My eyes get stuck on it
I can't get my eyes off it
Everything I do,
I can't get my eyes off it
I try and try but nothing works.

Blake Openshaw (9)
Sharples Primary School, Bolton

All About Me!

I am creative as Picasso,
My eyes are as brown as an old banana peel,
I am as generous as a doctor,
My favourite dessert is doughnuts,
My least favourite food is mashed potato,
My favourite book is by Tom Gates.

Aaminah Adam (9)
Sharples Primary School, Bolton

This Is My Life

I'm as fast as a cheetah when I play football.
My eyes are as blue as a bright crystal.
My hair is brown as the pitch-black, midnight sky.
I'm an animal lover, I love my German shepherd, he's really fluffy.

Dixon Henry (9)
Sharples Primary School, Bolton

This Is Me

Hi...
My name is Rebecca,
I'm a good rider,
I like the jumps higher and higher,
I love to trot,
Riding horses really rocks,
I love to gallop,
Galloping with my wild friend,
Every day,
Until the end,
This is me!

Rebecca Plumb (9)
St Edmund's RC Primary School, Bungay

This Is Me!

I'm as fast as a vampire,
Even faster than Sonic,
I'm a superstar striker in football,
I'm a lover of cats and dogs,
Bella, Max and Trisha are my favourites,
I'm as kind as kindness ever was and ever is,
I like making up jokes and riddles,
I like songs from Tick, Tick, Boom 30/90 by Andrew Garfield,
Here's a verse...
"They sing Happy Birthday,
You just want to lay down and cry,
Not just another birthday,
It's 30/90,
Why can't you stay 29?"
I like doing judo,
Today is my first day,
I'm as fearless as a Power Ranger,
When I'm angry, it's like I'm throwing a bomb that is about to explode,
Out of the window,

To keep my family safe,
When I go home on my scooter,
I sit on my sofa watching TV on the Sky box,
Watching Danger Force,
I'm a fan of Star Wars,
I like doing creative writing,
This is me!

Toby Bryant (8)
St Edmund's RC Primary School, Bungay

My Unique Recipe!

First add a drop of kindness,
Add a little passion too!
But maybe just sometimes a little bit of blue.
Put a lot of smartness,
With a pinch of silly powder,
Pluck the petals of a pretty flower.
My heart is a volcano of emotion,
Lots of tiger personality potion.
A flash of friendly and a squirt of awesome,
I love tigers they are so fluffy and pawsome!
Quarta bucket of anxiety and a pint of shyness too.
I may be different to people it's called unique
I am brave and I have lots of physique.
So this is me, I am proud and bold to be me!

Khadijah Sambou (10)
St James' CE Primary School, Oldbury

My Mum In A Cape

My mum is my superhero
And I love her very much.
Her cape is long and shiny
And lovely to touch.

No one else can notice her special cape
It's invisible to see
But with our magical powers
It's visible to me.

My mum is a superhero
She is as busy as a bee
Everything she does
Is to look after me.

With all the school runs
Chores and works for the NHS
My mum in a cape
Is as strong as a lioness.

Bradley Yates (9)
St James' CE Primary School, Oldbury

The Football Sport

I love to play football
Because it's very fun
But I hate it sometimes
Because I always have to
Dribble, dribble, dribble
To make the defender wibble
Right, left, right
The goal is in sight
I got a free-kick
But I am unfit
So I missed it
The crowd went crazy
But they threw a big daisy
Dribble, dribble, dribble
I made the defender wiggle.

Denzel Washington (10)
St James' CE Primary School, Oldbury

My Dream For The Future

H otels are the place
O f where there are rooms
T o make everyone say
E xcellent I should stay
L ovely things that I want to hear
S o that is what makes hotels so dear.

Akaalroop Singh (10)
St James' CE Primary School, Oldbury

Usagi The Space Snail

U sagi as you can see is very cute
S pace snail!
A little look makes you go awww!
G reat potential in this young space snail
I f I was in space I would find him!

Milo Alvarez (10)
St James' CE Primary School, Oldbury

This Is Who I Am

A s brave as a bear
N aughty as a raccoon
T all as a tree
O bedient as a dog
N ice as a cat
I ntelligent as a dolphin.

Antoni Oslawski (10)
St James' CE Primary School, Oldbury

A Tale Of Time

It started in prehistoric times,
Some creatures were like raptors I think
They said they only do tricks.
Stegos loved eating and never ever heating.
T-rexes were bad and always mad.
But they died and would never be revived.
On to a new era,
The Ice Age, never full of rage,
Mammoths big and strong,
They were never wrong.
Penguins, big, fat and are an inch taller than a cat
But sadly they were wiped out.
A new person called Jesus was born,
Only a boy, growing up to learn to tell about God,
He had a smart brain in his head,
And he was an adult.
He was put on a cross,
And blessed his friend called Ross.
Now at modern-day,
Always can find a way.
Planes higher than cranes,

Thousands of mean crimes and
That is the tale of time.

Ollie Rowtandson (10)
St John's Primary School, Liverpool

This Is Me And Who I Want To Be

I'm a very goofy,
Never back out of football,
And I'm kind of tall,
I'm in the mall,
Talking like a monster,
When I feel like I'm about to fall,
Here we go, just my luck,
I'm on a real football pitch,
In a real team,
Oh no, it's Liverpool.
I'll rather be thrown in a ditch,
Okay, too late,
I'm already in Everton.
Live life like a millionaire,
Drink some water then I find out I'm a striker star.
Oh no, I hit the floor but I'll be it one day.

Roman Masterson (9)
St John's Primary School, Liverpool

A Pet And A Vet

A pet was sick and needed some help,
And so it decided to yelp,
Its owner decided to take it to the vet,
And it was a bit of an angry pet.

As the vet looked to check it out,
The pet was thinking what is this about?
It stopped thinking for sure,
Because he looked like he was sure.

This is the last verse,
But the vet was the nurse,
It thought wrong,
But he was strong!

Kristina Pivkova (9)
St John's Primary School, Liverpool

My Name Is Myself

M y eyes are as blue as the ocean,
A mazing at kickboxing,
N eglective about English,
D ucks are my favourite animal,
Y ellow is my favourite colour.

H appy person,
U nderstands everything,
D oughnuts dipped in Nutella is my favourite snack,
S peedy in PE,
O utgoing with my friends,
N ever angry.

Mandy Hudson (10)
St John's Primary School, Liverpool

Joe Poem

J oyful Joe,
O n the go,
S low flow,
E merald crow,
P ossible overflow,
H igh but high low.

E arly snow,
V iolet outgrow,
A mazing dough,
N ot knowing though,
S mall review.

And that is my name.

Joseph Evans (10)
St John's Primary School, Liverpool

It's Just Me

I'm funny and always muddy.
I don't care that I'm always there.
I look in a puddle and the person I see,
Is me, me, me.
We are all the same,
So get it together and be happy like me!
This is just me, me, me.

Ruby Cuddy (9)
St John's Primary School, Liverpool

Toy

In a kingdom full of games,
When I thought of the toy.

Once upon a midnight smelly,
Deep into that darkness bidding,
By the grave, I saw the figurines,
Toy-tormentor of my dreams.

Theodore Ng (10)
St John's Primary School, Liverpool

This Is Me

I am a dancer,
Book reader,
Tennis player,
Summer gamer,
Chocolate eater,
Early riser,
Light sleeper,
Bread and jam maker,
A good helper.
I love maths.

Maneli Hashemi (9)
St John's Primary School, Liverpool

Stuff I Like

A n Everton fan,
I like hash browns,
D ixie Dean is the best Everton player,
A Beatles fan,
N o to Liverpool FC.

Aidan Jennings (10)
St John's Primary School, Liverpool

This Is Me

R eally kind.
I like maths.
L ove playing with a friend.
E xcellent boxer.
Y ellow is my favourite colour.

Riley Madden (10)
St John's Primary School, Liverpool

About Me

F unny and intelligent,
R ealistic,
E nergetic,
Y ells a lot,
A mazing.

Freya Cashman (11)
St John's Primary School, Liverpool

Flowers Of Personality

Each and every plant has its own personality and style
For example, you might have spiky hair, no worries
Because a cactus does too
You may smell lovely, lavender might relate
Roses are beautiful, don't you think
So are you
Most daisies are tiny, some might describe you, shortly like those daisies
Sunflowers are so bright, like the sun
While you might smell like the fresh scent of mint
Dandelions show elegance and dignity
Some may describe you as that
Blue iris symbolise these words
Faith, hope, wisdom and purity
Do you think that you are described this way
If so, do show curiosity to some
This may be very rare to find
Purple daisies show innocence and loyal love
You might be it too
The purple daisy also shows simplicity

The bird paradise shows love and you do that too
It also shows faithfulness and thoughtfulness
Geranium shows sensitivity, as you may.

Mia Tongson (8)
St Joseph's Catholic Primary School, Haywards Heath

This Is All About Me

I am like the sun, who tries to reach up to the top of the sky, every day
When I was born, I was a precious stone to my mum and dad
Four years later I was blessed with a lovely pretty sister
Then I became an elder son for my dad and mum
And a responsible elder brother to my lovely sister too...
So many years gone, I started schooling
My ambitions and goals have changed day by day
Today my aim is to study very well and to be a good footballer
I hope I can overcome the obstacles to achieve my goals
With the help of God Almighty
And thank you Lord for my beautiful life
I will be your lovely son for ever and ever.

Anold Johnson (9)
St Joseph's Catholic Primary School, Haywards Heath

How To Make Me

How do you make Florence?
One tablespoon of sweetness
Two of smartness, that will make a genius
A pinch of cuteness, we don't need rudeness

1000 grams of confidence, now that's a good sentence
Then add 85g of belief
And 10,000 handfuls of mischief
Now, just a little bit of was, or less
Okay, and five million tablespoons of gratefulness
And five grams of brightness
Now, add some miles, ones that you can see for miles
Don't forget the kindness
And that is sure to bring you happiness
And that is how you make Florence.

Florence Leppard (10)
St Joseph's Catholic Primary School, Haywards Heath

This Is Luis

Nine years ago, I was born
Already then, I was ready to score
Sport is my life and makes me happy
And I like to think that I am never snappy
I play football, rugby and I swim
But most of all I like to win
Scoring goals and tries I like
I also want to ride my bike
Going fast is really fun
And also when I'm on a run
I'm half English and half German
I also have a cousin, Herman
German, English, French I talk
Spanish I learn, when I'm on a walk
To play rugby is a treat
As long as there's not snow and sleet.

Luis Charlton (8)
St Joseph's Catholic Primary School, Haywards Heath

Me

Me, me, me!
What do you see?
Dark chocolate eyes, inky black hair,
And a lot of creativity.

My passion is art,
I love to express myself!
Splash some paint here,
A couple of sketches over there.

Oh, I just want to read books,
Glorious pages of words and words,
Losing myself in another's world.

Proud of my imperfection,
Learning along the way,
I make mistakes and I have my flaws,
But...
I love myself!

Jyothika Banesh (11)
St Joseph's Catholic Primary School, Haywards Heath

What I Dream To Be

I am a small human in a big world,
But size doesn't matter
I want to explore where hummingbirds hover
Maybe find a fossil or two
I want racism to end
And let the gods bend our world to a better place

My dream is to own a palaeontology centre
And discover a new dinosaur
And discover the undiscovered
Without wandering to another person's left
Lastly, I will give my brother half of my earnings
And help my family.

Alice Hartin (10)
St Joseph's Catholic Primary School, Haywards Heath

Super Max

The track of Silverstone,
The seats are filling up,
The engines are roaring,
The fire red lights are out.

Driver thirty-three, the fastest of them all,
If you don't let him pass,
He can cut through the grass.

Standing on the podium,
Verstappen is on top,
Hamilton is moaning,
Red Bull has won.

Luke Singanallur (10)
St Joseph's Catholic Primary School, Haywards Heath

A Place That Makes Me Happy

S hells sparkle beneath the soft sand,
O cean waves glisten in the summer sun,
P ebbles sinking under my feet,
H ard wet sand at the water's edge,
I ce cream melting in my hand,
E asily the most perfect day.

Sophie Duncan (10)
St Joseph's Catholic Primary School, Haywards Heath

The Heart I Have

The heart I have is unique,
The heart I have is like an antique,
Some people say I'm a freak,
But I think I'm cute and petite.

The heart I have is like gold,
But I love to stand out, bold.
I sometimes do what I'm told.

Keeran Espinosa (11)
St Joseph's Catholic Primary School, Haywards Heath

My School

I like to go to my school
I like to talk to my teachers
I like to read my books
I like to talk to my friends
I like to spend time in school
My school is my world and enjoyment
I love my school.

Kevin Mathew Lukose (9)
St Joseph's Catholic Primary School, Haywards Heath

This Is Me

My life is like a dream.
Life passes like a stream.
Time flies like a bird.
When I sleep, I enter a different world,
I get wings and fly away, far away, whoosh!

My life is like a book, that starts and ends.
The inside of my book is calm, funny, and adventurous.
When I am happy, I'm a ray of sunshine.
I'm a raging sea when I'm angry.
I am a raincloud when I am sad.
I am I, I focus on me.
You are you, so focus on you.
Be strong, be brave.

Arabella Luyimbazi (9)
St Joseph's Catholic Primary School, Deptford

This Is Me!

I have a dream to be an architect, I love art.
My favourite colour is blue, just like I like things new.
My skin is amazing, I like gazing.
I like myself, but I don't like being by myself.
I am kind in my mind.

My family is loving, bullies are not loving.
I love sweets, they make me smile.
Be proud just like me.

Be helpful, be delightful,
Be happy and have a positive life.

Summer Pham (9)
St Joseph's Catholic Primary School, Deptford

This Is Me, As You Can See

- **I** am proud of me
- **Z** ero of being scared
- **U** seful for helping others
- **C** heerful every day
- **H** elpful to friends and family
- **U** nbelievable heart
- **K** ind to others
- **W** ish for everyone to live a happy life
- **U** seful for helping others who are in need.

Izuchukwu Ohanenye (10)
St Joseph's Catholic Primary School, Deptford

Match Day

I wake up early, put on my kit
I can hardly contain my excitement to sit
It's time to go, we get in the car, I really hope it's not too far
We arrive, the team is here, a win for us today would make us cheer
The whistle blows, the game begins, all the supporters start to sing
This is my happy place, a massive smile appears on my face
Then we score, the crowd goes wild, and think to myself, I'm a very lucky child
That night in bed, the day going round in my head
I wonder when will be the next match day for me?

Tom Suttle (8)
St Mark's CE Primary School, Swanage

Me

I am seven, going on eight
V ery independent
Y ear three in St Mark's

R oses are my favourite flower
O ranges I like
S pinach I don't like
E llyn is my best friend.

Ivy Rose Goode (7)
St Mark's CE Primary School, Swanage

Cricket

I like cricket
I hit wickets
I have fun
And I score runs.

Bradley Wellman (7)
St Mark's CE Primary School, Swanage

This Is Me

I'm a strong, super great football machine
I'm a creative kid and amazing at art
I'm an awesome gaming god at games
I'm a Connect 4 champ
I'm as brave as a bear
And I'm as strong as a truck
I'm as nice as my mum
And my hair's as dark as the pen I'm using
I'm a supreme shooter at basketball
And I'm a god with the ball
This is me.

Ahmad Akbar (10)
St Mary's CE Primary School, Willesden

This Is Me!

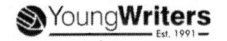

This is me
I am good at football
I play it with my friends
My brother is the best, he brightens up my day
I love my mother more than anything
As I gaze into the stars
This is me.

Riley Ranger (10)
St Mary's CE Primary School, Willesden

This Is Me

I have beautiful eyes like a shooting star in the dark night sky,
I am also as awesome as music can be,
I am as passionate as a horse galloping in the sea,
I am also as funny as an elephant dancing in a circus sea,
I am as enthusiastic as a novelist can be.

I am as energetic as a cheetah running around,
I have disliked spiders all my life,
I am as fun as a clown dancing about,
I am very competitive all the time.

I am as kind as a nurse can be,
I am also as helpful as a doctor,
But my biggest dream is to be a teacher,
And just be me.
This is me!

Olivia Michie (9)
St Mary's Primary School, Larkhall

Football

F ast speedy feet.
O ut up in the air.
O utside playing football with my friends.
T ogether we play football every day.
B et you can't score my feet are all over the place.
A bird came along to play with us.
L ike what I like.
L iving with me and football we will be better.

Lily Bailey (9)
St Nicholas CE Primary School, Henstridge

Who Am I?

I am Oliver,
I love to rock,
Football scorer,
Roblox gamer,
A dog boy,
Great swimmer,
Great artist,
I love cupcakes,
Funny human,
Good friend.

This is me.

Oliver Traves (9)
St Nicholas CE Primary School, Henstridge

Who's My Favourite Pokémon?

They are big and strong
They're grey
They're a Machop's evolution

Who is my favourite Pokémon?

Answer: A Machoke.

Zachary Peckover (8)
St Nicholas CE Primary School, Henstridge

This Is Me (Logan)

A kennings poem

I am Logan
I am a sweet eater
A teddy hugger
A gamer
A toy player
A pizza eater.

Logan Sunley (8)
St Nicholas CE Primary School, Henstridge

This Is Me

K ind and caring
A love of macaroni
R eally love to laugh and joke
L oath the thought of homework

H appy to help, no matter what
E nergetic is my middle name
R eady to be a mischief-maker
B ob the dog, my fearless friend
E xcited by the sight of snow
R oblox is my escapism.

Karl Herber (10)
St Peter's CE Primary School, South Weald

This Is Me!

A sensational swimmer,
The cold water gliding against my body,
Getting lost in a world of underwater magic.

Waking up early for an unforgettable holiday,
Hot air blowing against my cheeks ready for the beach,
Waves crashing over and over again.

Soggy cereal waiting to be eaten, yuck!
Off to the bin, it goes!
The poor spoon...

Sienna Neroni (11)
St Peter's CE Primary School, South Weald

This Is Me!

I am an...
Amazing animal lover, always looking after dogs,
The irritating sound of pots and pans,
Spending time with family and friends,
Not wanting to eat something I don't like,
Crazy chocolate and pizza lover,
Trying to find space as I walk through a crowd of people,
A big bookworm,
And finally...
A dancer!

Carlotta Strachan (11)
St Peter's CE Primary School, South Weald

This Is Me
A kennings poem

I am a...
Succulent steak lover,
Man United stalker,
Cheese hater,
Football fanatic,
Pepsi Max guzzler,
Running machine racer,
Chocolate muncher,
Pizza picker,
Dancing rival,
Snack pincher,
Boxing puncher,
Dog walker,
Reading revolter,
Goal scorer.

Alfie Kinnear (10)
St Peter's CE Primary School, South Weald

This Is Me!

I am a...
Dumpling diner,
Speedy racer,
Good guitar player,
Wildlife reserve admirer,
Pro Xbox gamer,
Artistic artist and art maker,
Book hoarder and reader,
Morning snooze taker,
Hand dryer hater,
Literature lover,
Writing habit owner,
And a massage master!

Henry Greenwood (9)
St Peter's CE Primary School, South Weald

This Is Me

T errific dog lover
H ates tuna
I biza fan
S hopping queen

I am not a fan of netball
S assy Clueless fan

M ake-up model
E legant Coco Chanel lover.

Sienna Kinnear (9)
St Peter's CE Primary School, South Weald

My Life

M y obsession with skateboarding
Y ou wouldn't believe how much

L ove the spicy life
I am a plain pizza guy
F amily fun
E specially when it comes to mind-jiggling jigsaws.

George Hirst (9)
St Peter's CE Primary School, South Weald

This Is Me

I am loyal

A mazing at making friends
M y life is a dream

L ove my family
O ne good person
L oyal to my friends
A stonishing at making people happy.

Lola Llewellyn (11)
St Peter's CE Primary School, South Weald

My Spectacular Story!

I am...
I am a fan of reading,
I am a lover of sleeping,
I am a sunset starer,
I am a lover of warm weather,
I am a fan of puppies and kittens,
I am a person for warm woollen mittens,
I am Jenna!

Jenna Shaybany (11)
St Peter's CE Primary School, South Weald

This Is Me!
A kennings poem

I am a...
Relaxed reader,
Lego lover,
Chocolate eater,
Excellent hugger,
Disney dreamer,
Summer enjoyer,
And finally...
A brilliant big brother.

Jaydon Purewal (10)
St Peter's CE Primary School, South Weald

This Is Me!
A kennings poem

I am a...
Football player,
Dog lover,
Cat hater,
Pudding lover,
Fast runner,
School hater,
Winter lover,
Summer hater.

Sonny McCarthy-Whitrod (9)
St Peter's CE Primary School, South Weald

How To Make Me

To make me you will need:
A small dog called Shep that is also plant-based,
A Nintendo Switch,
15g of fun,
A dollop of sleep,
An excellent swimmer,
A pinch of lasagne.

First, add the small, black dog called Shep to the frying pan,
Leave until golden brown.
Then get a Nintendo Switch,
And cut into 1cm slices,
Then place on top of the fried, small, black dog called Shep.
Then get 15g of fun and a dollop of sleep and roll into a bread roll.
Leave in the oven for 15 minutes,
Then get an excellent swimmer and a pinch of lasagne and make Krabby Patties.
Put in the oven.
This is burger me.

Joshua Harrison (10)
The Bluecoat School, Stamford

This Is Me

To make me you will need:
10lbs of fun,
1lbs of smarts,
1 piece of lasagne,
1lb of flour,
1 meatball
1 ice cube
1 dab of hot sauce.

First, get a pound of flour in a bowl.
Mix it for one minute.
Add a dab of hot sauce and put one ice cube in
Wait for the ice cube to melt.
Then add the meatball and lasagne then mix for 60 seconds.
Add 3lb of fun and put in the smarts and *boom!* This is me.

James Eason (9)
The Bluecoat School, Stamford

Bob!

You need to be organised,
Smart and artistic, and be ten years old,
And have ginger hair.
Favourite colour had to be the rainbow,
And like dogs, not kitties, and not a cat, either.
Wants to fly with a jetpack when older,
And like Hulk, and be a boy.
Cook yourself for fifty seconds, but with vinegar,
And you become me and you need to be,
Artistic.

Lawrence Buckingham (10)
The Bluecoat School, Stamford

This Is Me

I'm a...
Night owl,
Gamer,
Like swimming,
I'm Polish,
I like cars,
I play on Roblox,
I'm shy,
I like cats,
My favourite animal is a wolf,
I have one brother, two sisters,
I go on my laptop, tablet, and Xbox,
I'm smart and brave,
And finally,
I like art!

Adi Siwik (10)
The Bluecoat School, Stamford

All About Me

I adore swimming
I love to make friends
Lavender and ivory are my favourite colours
I feel blue sometimes... but that's okay!
I do sleep like a lion
I have a lovely family, and that's all I need
If that's not good enough you've lost your mind!
This is me!

Audrey Mugonda (10)
The Bluecoat School, Stamford

This Is Me!

I am...
Friendly as a dog,
Happy as the colour lavender,
Loving animals like a vet,
Hungry like a wolf,
Playful as a fox,
Sporty as a football player,
As messy as a pig,
As kind as a cat,
I am a night owl.
This is me.

Tegan Pell (10)
The Bluecoat School, Stamford

This Is Me

I love swimming.
You know I enjoy running.
Beware my funny personality,
It's crazy and deadly,
So if that's not enough,
You must be dreaming.

Macee Edwards-Jensen (10)
The Bluecoat School, Stamford

This Is Me

A spoonful of Fortnite,
A dash of football,
A measure of sport,
A gallon of annoying,
A litre of sarcasm,
This is me.
That's all!

Isaac Cowper (11)
The Bluecoat School, Stamford

This Is Me!

I am...
A crazy person,
Like TV,
Love trains,
A worrier
Adore tractors
Chocolate eater
Game player
This is me.

Kohle De Havilland (10)
The Bluecoat School, Stamford

Friends Forever

B esties forever
E ager to see each other
S afely helpful
T errific and nice

F riendly to each other
R estless, happy to help
I ndependent sometimes
E xcellently treated
N ever broke up from friendship
D angerous but only a tiny bit
S ad not really that much.

Jayden Barnes (9)
Thomas Whitehead CE Academy, Houghton Regis

My Favourite Food

C hristmas is the best for me
H ot chocolate is the best for me
O utside is very refreshing for me
C oco is the best movie for me
O range is the best for me
L imo is big for me
A nyone is the best, even me
T owels are the best, they dry me
E very person is in my house.

Crystal Hall (8)
Thomas Whitehead CE Academy, Houghton Regis

Fun Facts About Harry

H aving fun is what I like
A chieving hard problems
R acing is what I do
R unning is my thing
Y ellow is one of my favourite colours

B londe, light hair
E agle eyes
N o slowing down
S upersonic power
O n task every time
N othing stops me.

Harry Benson-Coleman (7)
Thomas Whitehead CE Academy, Houghton Regis

Rhys Bennett

R abbit lover
H at wearer
Y es, give me chocolate every day
S ometimes play outside with my friend

B est school ever!
E at now!
N ever liked nature
N oodles are yummy and edible
E than is my friend
T ests are hard!
T Vs are huge.

Rhys Bennett (8)
Trinity Academy, Richmond

All About Abdullah

Haiku poetry

I am very fast,
Because I practice a lot,
So I always win.

Reading is my thing,
Go ahead and read a book,
Get smart by reading.

Riding bikes is fun,
Get fit by exercising,
Biking always fun.

Doctors help people,
Choose a doctor that is smart
So come and choose me.

Abdullah Qumi (8)
Valley Invicta Primary School At East Borough, Maidstone

Oliver

I am the footballer spirit inside my heart
I'm Liverpool FC, winning the Champions League
I am the unique branch, sprouting from my family tree
I love cricket and my reflexes are as quick as a cheetah
I am a master at being a midfielder
I am a maths whizz, solving calculations faster than a rocket
I love drawing and writing and enjoy it
I am at Wilberlee Junior and Infant school.

Oliver Zahoor (10)
Wilberlee Junior & Infant School, Wilberlee

The Poem Of Me

I am Isaac Bennett
I am the ground that keeps the buildings standing
I am as cunning as a cat
I am the pencil that hits the paper
I am a gamer
I am a thinker
I am a builder of Lego
I am a drink of sweet hot chocolate
I am as fast as a cheetah
I am who I want to be.

Isaac Bennett (11)
Wilberlee Junior & Infant School, Wilberlee

Me

This is me,
I am who I want to be,
When I'm having fun, time flies,
And my favourite food is fries.

When I'm with my friends, the time never ends,
And all that is ever broken, mends,
I am proud of who I am,
If anyone is rude, I don't give a damn!

I am unique in my own ways,
But my life is like a maze,
Sometimes, it isn't very easy,
But at least it's not like this poem - cheesy!

Doyinsola Abdul-Obitayo (12)
Wymondham College, Morley

YoungWriters Est. 1991

YOUNG WRITERS INFORMATION

We hope you have enjoyed reading this book – and that you will continue to in the coming years.

If you're the parent or family member of an enthusiastic poet or story writer, do visit our website **www.youngwriters.co.uk/subscribe** and sign up to receive news, competitions, writing challenges and tips, activities and much, much more! There's lots to keep budding writers motivated!

If you would like to order further copies of this book, or any of our other titles, then please give us a call or order via your online account.

Young Writers
Remus House
Coltsfoot Drive
Peterborough
PE2 9BF
(01733) 890066
info@youngwriters.co.uk

Join in the conversation!
Tips, news, giveaways and much more!

YoungWritersUK YoungWritersCW youngwriterscw